written by
Tracy Blom

Illustrated and Designed by
Fx and color Studio

Rumors and questions flew through the zoo.
"Is Ralph leaving again? Where will he go to?"
These were all questions Ralph had answers to.
He had drawn out a map and invited friends, too!

He needed someone he could easily take,
so he invited Sylvester the slithery snake.
Milo the monkey asked, "Mind if I tag along?
I can travel quite fast since my arms are so long."
Ollie the Ocelot called down from the tree,
"If you want someone fast, then you should bring me."

"We'll need to blend in, or they'll find us," Ralph said.
As Milo the monkey put a hat on his head
They found some old clothes in the lost and found.
Ralph put on a jacket with the snake tied around.
Milo found a cape to go with his hat,
and stood on the back of the ocelot cat.

They ran through the city towards a big flashing sign,
found the train labelled "London" and hopped right in line.

The train pulled into the station, and the doors opened wide.
The first stop on their journey was a Ferris wheel ride.
They bought their tickets and soared through the sky,
aboard the famous London Eye.

Next, they went to a big famous clock,
but someone bumped Milo as they started to walk,
and Milo fell off of Ollie's head.
"Stop those animals!" somebody said.

Ollie said, "We need somewhere to hide!"
Ralph saw a museum and ran right inside.
Sylvester posed like a drawing up on the wall.
Milo climbed an obelisk and sat really tall.
Ollie found a statue that looked just like him.
And Ralph, well … he just couldn't fit in.

**A guard walked in and shined his light
on something quite tall that didn't look right.
"Hm, I don't remember seeing that there,"
he said to the pharaoh with the long golden hair.**

Ralph politely said, "should we not be in here?"
As the guard jumped back and screamed in fear,
"Alert! Alert! We have a code red!"
And as he yelled, the animals fled.

They came to a palace with guards dressed in red.
They stood really still with big hats on their heads.
Milo walked to the gate and said, "Follow me."
And in no time at all, they were seated for tea.

The queen walked in and took her seat,
and looked over her guests, who sat nice and neat.
They laughed and talked for an hour or two,
but as they were leaving, the queen went, "Ahchoo!"
She blew off their disguises with one epic sneeze,
which caused all the animals to panic and freeze.

Ralph grabbed one more mouthful of grapes,
Milo ran for the door to make his escape,
Ollie made a break for the hall,
and Sylvester went, "Hisss!" and frightened them all.

The guards yelled, "Stop!" as the animals ran.
Ralph saw a bus coming and thought up a plan.
They hopped on board, since the next stop was the zoo,
and from the top deck they had the best view.

The sun began setting as they reached the zoo gate.
They got back in time, not a moment too late.
"We sure had fun, but wish you were there, too.
Maybe next time we can all leave the zoo!"

THE END

Copyright © 2020 by Tracy Blom

All rights reserved. No part of this publication may be reproduced, distributed, or transmitted in any form or by any means, including photocopying, recording, or other electronic or mechanical methods, without the prior written permission of the author, except in the case of brief quotations embodied in critical reviews and certain other noncommercial uses permitted by copyright law.

For permission requests regarding this story or illustrations, contact the author via her website:

www.theblomdotcom.com

Printed in the United States of America

First Printing, 2020

Made in the USA
Columbia, SC
28 August 2022